ADORATIONS

A POETIC EXPRESSION OF FAITH

Annwyl

Edited by: K Pynkynmawlang Syiemlieh
Book Cover Design: Saher, K Pynkynmawlang Syiemlieh
Illustrations by: Saher

Printed at Notion Press, India (POD)

*This work is dedicated to Jesus
"My Saviour and salvation"
and Auntie Jerri.*

Contents

Holy tree

When my life was a withered dying branch,
With no green leaves or happy flowers,
Woe begone and desolate, were both dusk and
dawn hours.

Then I looked at the Holy tree,
Adorned with flowers
Clothed in splendor and glory.

With every season in His leaves, shade from sun
and storms at His feet.

With face of light and fruit of delight,
Tree of life stood in numinous majesty.

I was a fallen branch of the tree,
To wither and burn was my fate to be.

But He looked at me in love and mercy and said:

"With me your place will be".

Branch belongs to the tree,
Blood of the Lamb gives life to me.

Jesus is the Holy tree,
Who will give life for eternity.

Bright and morning star

He always comes when the night seems darkest.
His strength is exceedingly great when I am at my
weakest.

After travelling in the wilderness,
He is the rest.
He cast away my sins,
As far away as east is from the west

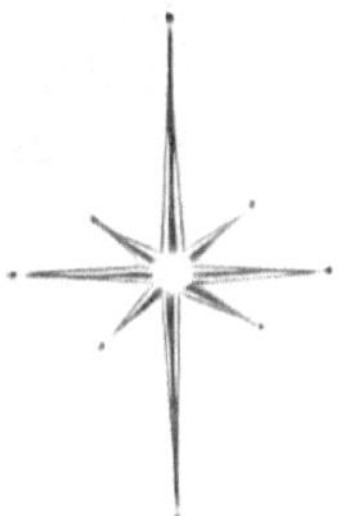

I will wait all my life for
His plans to unfold,
For He saves for last the best.

His love and light from me is never far,
He is Jesus,
The bright and morning star.

Ancient of days

God of mercy, compassion and Kindness,
Father who made us in His likeness.

King, in His beauty, took away my ugliness,
Cleaned me like morning dew,
Every hour, everyday, I am new.

Lord of time, Ancient of days,
Guiding light on dark, turbulent ways.

He shines through the clouds like golden sun rays.

His Kingdom lasts forever and more,
He is the Heaven's living door.

Lord of Lords

Lord of lords and King of kings,
of His Glory and Majesty,
The Heaven and earth sings.

Almighty God beyond compare,
Never far, always near.

If I go to heaven, He is there,
On earth, He is the one who took away my every
care.

His presence lights up the dawn so fair,
His image is reflected in every face that is kind
and dear.

God of faithfulness

After the weeping of the night,
You are my morning light, comforting and bright.
After a while of the despair of my heart,
You are my soul's eternal delight.

I searched the earth so vast,
In you, I found my hope at last.
You are the promisekeeper and the promise,
God of faithfulness, love unfailing, and steadfast.

Be still and know that He is God

God of all my days,
God of all my ways,
God of morning sunrays.

You are God when foundation of the earth
shakes,
You are God even when the
most mighty mountain breaks.

God of rest, my shield from
storms,
God of Hope in depths of despair,
God who heals the hearts in need of repair.

God who makes dead bones dance,
God who did not leave my life to chance.

Even when the sun, sky, and stars fall,
I will be still and know that you are God,
Jesus, King of Kings and Eternal Lord.

Salvation

I asked the Lord,
"only the righteous will inherit the promised land.
I am not Righteous or clean, my brokenness,
your Holy eyes have seen."

He replied

"I gave my life to take away your sin.
My righteousness belongs to you.
In my eyes, you are clean and new."

Now, of my salvation I am sure,
Your heart is my heart, clean and pure.

The great I am

He is the Healing and Salvation,
He is the King of every nation.

He is the morning star and light,
He is the righteous one, God of Might.

He is the unfailing love,
He is the promise of salvation from heaven
above.

He is the goodness and Holiness,
He is the comfort and companion in our
loneliness.

In Heaven or on earth, no power has any other
name.
He is 'The Great I AM'.

Always God

You are God of all my days,
You are God of all my ways,
You are God of morning sunrays.

You are found in dusk shadows,
You dwell in Spring meadows,
You are warmth in winter snows.

You are God of my youth,
You are still God in my last days,
You are God when I took my first breath,
You are still God at my last sigh,
You are the saviour who is always nigh.

Rose of Sharon

Lily of the valley,
Rose of Sharon.

Voice of Moses,
Righteousness of Aaron.

Fairer than the children of men,
You are God now, You were God then.

Good Shepherd of your sheep,
Your Love is heaven high,
Your faithfulness ocean deep.

Love

The most beautiful love story that was ever told;
Began When God was born on earth,
On a winter night so cold.

The greatest love story that is, or was,
Is Witnessed When you see Jesus on the Cross.

He is

He is the life and the light,
He is my heart's delight.

He is the lamb slain,
He is my treasure and gain.

He is the Lily of the valley and Rose of Sharon,
He brings spring to lands that are barren.

He is the first and the last,
Hope of the future and redemption of the past.

He is the good shepherd of His sheep,
He is my peace and restful sleep.

He is the God that provides,
He is my guiding light.

He is the God who is always near,
He is my strength in every fear.

He is the Lord of lords and the King of kings.

Redeemer

I was blind, but you have become the light of my
eyes,
You are the truth in the world of lies.

There is no death for me because my redeemer
lives,
God of Wonders,
New life to dead bones, He gives.

Bible

Bible is a letter of love,
Written to us by by our loving Father from
heaven above.

Bible is a song of grace,
That will last for endless days.

Bible is a story of Redemption,
To be proclaimed in every nation.

Bible is the place of rest,
That you will not find anywhere else,
If all the earth you search from east to west.

Name of Love

Holy, Holy, Holy, is He,
The eyes that cannot sin see.
Sovereign of the universe looked
At the wretched, sinful humanity and had mercy.

God almighty came to earth as a limited man,
And for our sin was slain.

Wages of our folly were His to be,
Death on the cross of the king.
The Heaven and earth did see!

Unfailing love will be named,
Jesus Christ, for eternity.

Promised Land

Your reflections are found in everything that is
beautiful and true,
Your colours adorn every dawn's golden hue.

You yourself are the serene green meadows,
and you are the fragrance of the rose.

Made of a little spark of your glory are the stars,
sun and the moon, Made of your smile are the
lilies of June.

You are the clear effervescent waters of peace,
And is summer, You are the cool-Shade of trees.

Clothed in splendor, majesty, and light,
Shelter is in your wings, be it day or night.

You are my portion, inheritance, and guiding
hand,
You, God most high, are the promised land.

Saviour of everyday

If I was saved a single time, a single day,
Soon I would fall again and lose my way.

But my God is mighty to save;
He is the saviour of every moment of everyday.

Even if the world is engulfed in darkness,
He is my everlasting light,
Saviour of the world, God of might.

In Him alone, my spirit will forever delight.

Perfect Man

Man of righteousness, man of Holiness,
Man of kindness who takes away the human
loneliness.

Man of humility, even when He is the eternal
King of kings.
Man of compassion, of His mercy Heaven and
earth sings.

Man of truth, grace, and light,
Man of patience, peace, and forgiveness,
Even though persecuted day and night.

Man of Love beyond measure,
Every word He spoke, an incomparable treasure.

If the eyes of the world seek a perfect man to see,
Jesus Christ of Nazareth will that be.

Everlasting God

On love of men, you cannot depend;
It changes like the fickle wind.

In favours of seasons, no one can rest their heart;
In the blink of an eye, they depart.

If your hopes are put in the golden dawn,
Within no time, it is gone.
Trust will fail if it is put in the night,
At the approach of first sun rays it takes flight.

There is only one unfailing love,
One who is faithful till the end.
One who is true even when we are false,
One who is unchanging in all His ways—
Eternal, everlasting God of ancient days.

God of mysterious ways

God who falls like rain on dry parched land,
God who shines like sunshine on cold winter
days,
God most high of mysterious ways.

God who comforts, His every child with a
broken heart,
God who raging oceans for his children did part.

God, who answers to every soul that prays,
God, the miracle of all our days.

Saviour

You saved me from afflictions and every fall,
When unto your name my broken heart did call.

You saved me from walking in the darkness of
the night,
When my steps you guided with your light.

You saved me from temptations, sin, and things
unseen,
Your blood shed on the cross made me clean.

All my days, you lead me with your staff and rod,
You are the only Living God.

He calls me His own

The dawn breaks into a song of His Glory,
The day sings of His unfailing love,
The rainbow and rain are of His beauty an eternal
story.

The Sun is a little glimpse the light of His face,
The winter sunshine a reminder of His warm
embrace.

The moon and the stars talk of the splendor of
His throne,
Every day of life makes His everlasting
faithfulness known,
He is the God who called me His own.

Protection of the King

Last night, I dreamt of peace and rest,
For which my whole life I searched, in east and
west.

I saw meadows of flowers and
butterflies,
A city devoid of hatred and lies.

My head rested in a lap of inexplicable comfort
and warmth,
I was secure and safe, and heard the angels sing,
I was in the protection of the most high God,
the Everlasting King.

God of beauty

When He smiles, flowers of spring bloom,
His presence takes away every heart's gloom.

His face is the sun shining in dark clouds,
He is the moon of hope in all my doubts.

Clothed in splendor and rainbow colors,
He is the companion of all my lonely hours.

With voice of a nightingale,
He calms all my fears,
With Him by my side, there
are no worries or cares.

His steps radiate beauty and
grace,
His chariot is made of cooling
Shade.

God of beauty, majesty, and might.
Saviour God, King clothed in enchanting light.

Living God

When in a thousand pieces breaks the heart,
When all our lives fall apart,
When the very being falls to ground
like dust and sand,
The only one that can restore all we have lost
Collect all the Wandering dust and sand,
Is the Living God's Almighty Hand.

God of love

First rays of the sun bring soft
Whispers of His Love,
Soft as falling snow is His smile,
In His healing presence come and sit awhile.

Search In Earth below or heavens above or any
other place,
But never is found, the pure beauty of His face.

Full of Kindness and mercy is His gaze,
Which radiates unfathomable grace,
All creation sings His praise.

Belonging

Every time I fall, you are there to give me your
hand,
Every time I hide in the darkness in shame,
You are there with your light to guide me home.
Every time I forget who I am,
You are there to tell me, I belong to your Holy
name.

When I fall into the dark night,
Jesus is my dawn of light.

Every time I give up on myself you say
"I will never leave thee nor forsake thee".

I belong to you Lord,
My heart and life forever will yours be.

Potter's clay

I Am a work of His hands of His perfect plans.

Before I was born, He for Himself set me apart
His love for me will never depart.

I am the clay, He is the potter,
He gives me life, He is the living water.

My Life is a Story of His goodness and glory.

My lips will in morning and evening sing His
praise.
In the assembly of the world for endless days.

Prince of Peace

There is no rest in east or west,
In Slumbering dreams or sleeplessness.

No peace even if I drown in the ocean or to the
skies take flight.

There is no tranquility in darkness of the night,
Or in the golden day's light.

Peace, rest and quiet for the soul,
Everything that makes us whole,
Is not in shadows of trees or in seven seas,
Its all found at the feet of the Prince of Peace.

Creator God

You created the universe with your word,
You painted the night sky with glittering
shimmering stars.
You sculpted the mountains of the earth with
your mighty hands.
With, forests oceans and flowers you adorned the
lands.

You decorated the sky with the rainbow after rain,
Formed the mighty lion, graceful deer and the
beautiful peacock so fair.

Maker of every wonderful, beautiful thing,
You are the creator God Almighty King.

God of Amazing Grace

Troubles are many but your blessings are more,
Darkness is thick but your light shines brighter.

Despair might surround me, but you are the hope
of my heart.

Doubts are many but you are the surety of my
spirit,
You are my salvation, my most precious gift.

All the ways of the world might be closed,
But of your mercy I am sure,
You are the gate, heaven's open door.

Sins and falls are many but there is forgiveness in
the light of your face,
You are the God of amazing grace.

God my miracle

Looking for wonders from east to west,
Looking for lands with peace and rest.

Chasing for rainbows and fool's gold,
Trying to find joy in future plans,
Or memories of old.

Wanting a miracle day and night in the songs of
the day and lullaby of the stars bright.

I did seek all this in vain,
Then I looked at your face and every treasure
I did gain.

He is the most precious gift that I found,
In Him joy forever does abound.

You are the one who broke my chains,
And sin's shackle, you yourself are God my
miracle.

King of Glory

When all my days became futile and empty,
My spirit questioning is this how my life will be?

I had no answer but the God of wisdom spoke to
me.
He said
" My grace is enough for everyday, I have
ordained for thee.
My glory in your life you will still see."

His every promise is true,
Store of His strength and grace it never gets
empty.
His goodness and glory in every passing day I do
see.
Never again has my spirit been empty.

God who remembers

I thought in the wilderness
There will no shade be for me
He said
 "I am the God who sees, I Myself will your
shade be"

I thought in the valley of the shadow of death
Who will listen to my cry of agony?
He said
"I am the God who hears, I will save you from
every trouble and will your guiding light be."

I looked at myself and saw my scarred wounded
heart,
I thought, there will never any healing be.
He said
"I am the God who heals, I will heal your spirit
and body.
In the land of the living My goodness you will
see."

In my lonely hours I thought I am forgotten and
no one cares for me.
He said
"I have carved your name on the palm of my
hand.
I am the God who remembers,
I will give life to your fading embers."

Garden of the Lord

Lord's garden is so fair,
With tulips of mercy and sunflowers
Of kindness born in a pair.

Rows of jasmine of compassion,
That spreads His goodness to every
nation.

Lofty Cedars of protection and shade,
Roses of beauty in every glade.

Rivers of wisdom nourish your flowers and trees,
Sunlight of goodness for every seed of hope.

Lilies of love sprout in every corner,
Every new dawn sings in your honour.

You, Yourself are the tree of life in the centre,
Your salvation and faithfulness always near,
Lord, Your Garden is so fair.

Hope

In the world of constant despair,
There is Hope in Jesus who will always care.

In the days of incessant fear,
Courage of the most High God is always there.

In the nights of forlorn darkness,
When everything is unclear,
God of light, lights my way,
He is always near.

God of patience

He waited till I got tired of my wandering ways.

He still looked at me with kindness,
As I squandered my nights and days.

His wings shielded me when I walked on perilous
roads,
When with hostility by every tongue my name
was called,
He still had for me kind words.

Even though come and go seasons and rise and
fall nations,
He is the everlasting, unchanging King, my God
of Patience.

Lamb Slain

He is the Lion of the tribe of Judah,
Almighty King who forever reigns,
But for my sake, He became the lamb slain,
So I could be free from sin, death, and pain.

Victory

In Him no hatred was found,
When on the tree of Calvary,
His hands were bound.
No King Like Him, is or was,
He did not fight with violence but won with love,
When He sacrificed Himself on the cross.

Acknowledgement

From the Author,

I must begin by thanking God and my wonderful family:

Jonathan Luke Smith and Jerri Smith : Your life is an inspiration to live a life of faithfulness to God.

Papa: You are a source of inspiration for me, and you have taught me to believe in myself.

Mom: You have taught me to be strong and tender while also inspiring me to make my dreams come true.

Mary: For all the smiles you gave me on all my ideas for genuine feedback and ideas of improvement.

Dan: For all the tough love. Without it, I would be too laidback to get anything done

Rabecca: For always being there to proofread for me, for assisting me in regaining confidence, and for your faith in me to complete my work.

Saher: For the cover art and all the pictures, for being the perfectionist and inspiring perfection in me.

Fr. Anthology Melvis: For being the reflection of God's light during my darkest days.

To Pynkynmaw: Without your help this book would hardly be possible.

To Sanjeev Kumar Saha: For motivating me daily to not give up.

To Nehchal: For always being ready to help in all ways to make this possible.

About the author

Annwyl is a poet, and this is her debut book, written in a poetic style that will inspire those who appreciate great creativity and true art.

She expresses her feelings through poems.

This book is her poetic expression of her worship and adoration for Jesus.

Contact Information

Email: annwyl84@gmail.com